Tiddlers

Splash!

by Damian Harvey

Illustrated by Sam Hearn

FRANKLIN WATTS
LONDON • SYDNEY

Notes on the series

TIDDLERS are structured to provide support for children who are starting to read on their own. The stories may also be used for sharing with children.

Starting to read alone can be daunting. **TIDDLERS** help by listing the words in the book for a check before reading, and by providing visual support and repeating words and phrases. These books will both develop confidence and encourage reading and rereading for pleasure.

If you are reading this book with a child, here are a few suggestions:

1. Make reading fun! Choose a time to read when you and the child are relaxed and have time to share the story.
2. Talk about the story before you start reading. Look at the cover and the blurb. What might the story be about? Why might the child like it?
3. Look also at the list of words below - can the child tackle most of the words?
4. Encourage the child to retell the story, using the jumbled picture puzzle.
5. Give praise! Remember that small mistakes need not always be corrected.

Here is a list of the words in this story.

Common words:

and	mum	said
but	of	the
get	out	to
I		

Other words:

bath	puddles	splish
hate	rain	time
love	splash	yuk

"I hate rain!"

Splish! Splash!
Splish! Splash!

"But I love puddles."

Splish! Splash!
Splish! Splash!

"Get out of the puddles," said Mum.

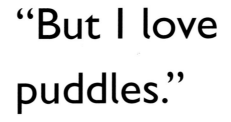

13

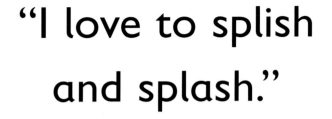

"Bath time," said Mum.

"Yuk! I hate baths."

Splish! Splash!
Splish! Splash!

Puzzle Time

Can you find these
pictures in the story?

Which pages are the pictures from?

Turn over for answers!

Answers

The pictures come from these pages:

a. pages 8-9

b. pages 20-21

c. pages 16-17

d. pages 10-11

First published in 2012 by
Franklin Watts
338 Euston Road
London
NW1 3BH

Franklin Watts Australia
Level 17/207 Kent Street
Sydney
NSW 2000

Text © Damian Harvey 2012
Illustration © Sam Hearn 2012

The rights of Damian Harvey to be
identified as the author and Sam Hearn
as the illustrator of this Work have been
asserted in accordance with the Copyright,
Designs and Patents Act, 1988.

A CIP catalogue record for this book is
available from the British Library.

ISBN 978 1 4451 0685 4 (hbk)
ISBN 978 1 4451 0691 5 (pbk)

Series Editor: Jackie Hamley
Editor: Melanie Palmer
Series Advisor: Catherine Glavina
Series Designer: Peter Scoulding

Printed in China

Franklin Watts is a division of Hachette Children's Books,
an Hachette UK company. www.hachette.co.uk

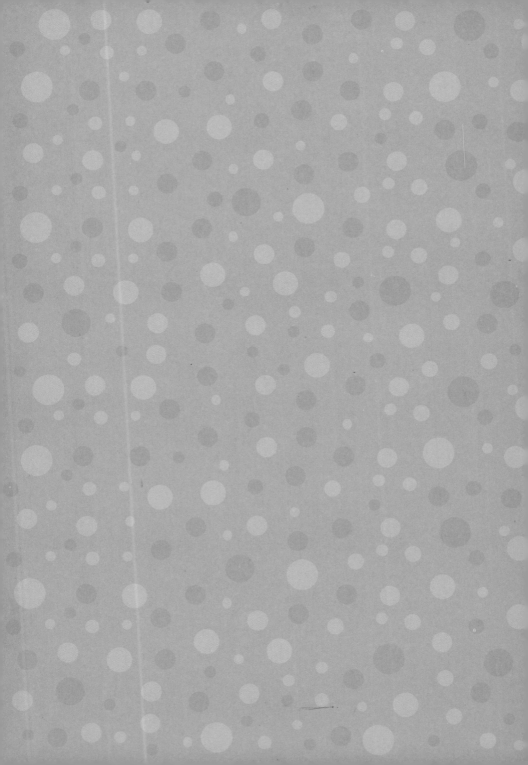